The Potato Ea

The train pulled into Cambridge station four minutes early. It was of no consequence other than that its driver had time to light a cigarette and take a few puffs. Maybe he had a pipe. You don't see many pipe smokers these days. Assuming he smoked at all, of course. It made no difference to me and allowed a little extra time to find a window seat without jostling those with the same idea. As it happened, I found a place in the first carriage to my left and settled in as comfortably as a

British train allowed. I could have paid extra and enjoyed the luxury of a first-class seat but I don't have money to burn.

*

The compartment filled quite rapidly but, strangely, nobody chose to sit beside me. I'd sprayed myself with a great-smelling anti-deodorant before setting out that morning, so I guess I simply struck lucky. In fact, it was three stations down the line before I had company.

"Sorry to disturb your peace," the newcomer said by way of introduction.

2

"The train's really crowded this morning."

I'm not best-known for my geniality but I nodded and offered a tight smile by way of a response.

"Going all the way?" I asked hopefully and wished for a negative reply.

"I never do things by halves," he responded. "All the way, young man. All the way."

After a couple of minutes the silence started to become embarrassing.

"My name's James but you can call me

Jimmy," the stranger announced.

This placed me under an obligation to respond.

"Francis," I half-muttered.

"Francis? I knew a girl once called Francis."

Was I expected to provide a witty response?"

"Pretty lass, too. She could drink anyone under the table. Sad ending, though. She drank herself under a car crossing a busy road."

I glanced surreptitiously at my watch.

"Am I boring you?" Jimmy asked.

"Oh … no, not at all," I replied guiltily.
"I'm expecting a call at ten-thirty. I just
wondered what the time was."

"Sorry. The fault's mine. You must think I
sounded rude."

"Not at all," I responded. I wasn't
expecting a call. I've no idea why I felt the
need to lie.

"You're not a very good liar," Jimmy
chuckled. "I've a tricky day ahead and my

nerves are getting the better of me."

"And now you're putting my curiosity to the test," I said. "If you're going all the way to London then I can fully understand your anxiety. Negotiating London is a pet hate of mine."

"Really?" Jimmy looked at me as if I'd said something quite ludicrous.

"I do most of my business in town. Know it like the back of my hand."

"May I ask what sort of business it is?"

"Not today you can't, sonny. I talk too

much."

I bridled at the term '*sonny*' but kept my mouth shut.

*

The train rattled on. Thirty minutes and half the journey completed.

My eyelids felt heavy. I think I was on the point of falling asleep when I was aware of two thickset, somewhat brutish-looking men approaching. I'm just five feet four and anyone three inches taller looks intimidating. These men were taller than that and broad-chested. If I didn't know better I'd take them for hoodlums but then what do I know.

The two men drew level. One continued past and along the carriage to a connecting door. The other stopped and whispered something in Jimmy's ear. Jimmy nodded and put a finger to his lips. I'd quite made up my mind that I wouldn't want to bump into these guys on a dark night. Not that it was likely, of course, was it?

*

The train drew into King's Cross and its passengers began gathering their belongings and moving towards the doors. The gangway was very soon congested and I steeled myself for a tedious wait and a slow shuffle towards an exit door. There was no way I was going to force my way into the queue. I'm only five feet four and no hero.

I was on the point of sitting down again and waiting for the queue to pass when a heavy hand landed on my shoulder.

"On your feet, sonny, or you'll be here all day."

It was Jimmy and he held a muscular arm

wide to prevent the other passengers from moving forward.

I rose from my seat, shrugged my shoulders and mumbled apologies to those trapped behind the thug's arm. I call him a thug because my judgement of him was becoming less benign by the minute.

I felt like a sandwich filling squashed between two thick slices of bread as I shuffled forward.

As I stepped down on to the platform, I felt something dig into my back. I was

about to turn around but changed my mind
when a voice in my ear whispered,

"Just keep looking straight ahead, Francis,
and you won't get hurt."

I won't get hurt? What the hell…?

I shuffled along the platform, one
muscular loony in front of me and Jimmy
immediately behind. I glanced sideways
and caught a third hoodlum grinning at
me. So, what was the joke? I wasn't about
to break out laughing.

*

11

My plan had been to visit a music publisher in Camden. Its offices were in Pancras Square, just a short walk from Kings Cross station. I had a couple of new songs to offer. I didn't think my new companions would want to go with me. Frankly, I began to think they'd no intention of letting me go anywhere without them. A few moments later this supposition was borne out when a large, sleek black car pulled up alongside and the back door was flung open.

"Inside," one of the thugs ordered. I was not about to argue with him.

I scrambled onto the back seat and was quickly joined by two of the hoodlums. Jimmy joined the driver in the front.

This was not turning out to be quite the day I had expected it to be when setting out from Cambridge that morning. I'd started the day as a free man but now felt a prisoner.

"Where are we going?" I asked.

Jimmy twisted round in his seat.

"Too many questions," he replied.

I'd only asked *one* question!

13

*

We must have travelled for close on an hour before the car slowed. Not a single word had passed between the car's occupants following my enquiry regarding our destination. I was feeling tired and hungry. A can of *Coke* would have gone down well, too.

And then … surprise, surprise! I felt the car slow. It pulled over to the left and then made a further sharp turn onto a farm track. We bumped along for several hundred metres before pulling up in front of a dilapidated farmhouse.

14

"Are we home?" I asked light-heartedly.

"For the time being," Jimmy replied, "but don't expect your mummy to be waiting for you with a cup of tea and a biscuit."

He and I did not share the same sense of humour.

*

"You'll stay here tonight," Jimmy informed me over fish and chips that one of his cronies had gone out and bought for our evening meals.

That and a Coke went down well but I couldn't help wishing I was enjoying them in my own flat in preference to this old farmhouse.

"What do you want with me? What good am I to you as a hostage?"

Jimmy laughed.

"You're not our hostage. We have some business to attend to and we can't have you shooting off your mouth to the police."

"Telling them what exactly?"

"Telling them that we're in town. Where we are. Giving them our descriptions."

"But I don't know where we are. Okay - somewhere out in the wilds at the end of a farm track - but that's all."

A sudden thought struck me - one I should have given voice to way back at the beginning of this unfortunate adventure.

"What are you up to?" I asked bluntly.

"You don't want to know," one of my abductors called out. They called him Franky.

"I *do* want to know. My friends, my family … they will have reported me missing."

"Fair point," Franky said. "I'll let them all know that you're enjoying a few days' solitude in the countryside."

"Solitude?"

"Quiet thinking time away from the rat race," Franky replied. "Dreaming up a new song, if you like."

"They know I came up on a train to London specifically to sell a couple of *old* songs," I countered.

"And we told them you changed your plans after you got on the train."

18

"And just how could you possibly have done that?"

Jimmy grinned at me.

"Frank's a useful member of my small team. He's pretty nifty with his fingers."

"That doesn't answer my question."

Jimmy walked over to me.

"Let me explain. You have seventeen friends on *Facebook*. Your sister lives in Penzance. Your parents in Dover. You've already mentioned one of your hobbies is song writing. You also belong to a

19

rambling club … so do you want me to go on?"

He must have noticed the look of incredulity on my face.

"How do you know all this?"

"Franky used his nifty fingers to borrow your *iPhone* as you left the train back in London."

*

I checked the pockets of the jacket I'd worn on my train journey down to London. My *iPhone* was missing. It must have been Franky that I felt brush against me as we stepped down from the train and onto the platform. How could I have been so stupid not to have noticed? These men now had details of all my contacts. If they had explored the contents of my phone then they might well have discovered …

"We found some interesting photos on your phone," Franky told me. "Quite a pretty girl, don't you agree? Well, of course you do! Sorry … silly question."

"That's none of your business," I retorted.

"No, of course not. You're quite right. It

might be of interest to the police, though. Do you think I should give them a call? Ask their opinion?"

My head began to throb. How could I have been so stupid? I should have deleted the selfies Sophie sent me.

"Or I could upload them to *Facebook*, *Whatsapp* and *X*, I suppose, and serve up a treat for your followers."

"I'd rather you didn't," I replied somewhat lamely.

"Hmm. We'll see. Actually, there might be a way out for you."

22

I hesitated, wondering just what that '*way out*' might be.

"Anyway, that's something we can talk about in the morning."

"In the morning?" I spluttered. "You mean I have to stay here tonight?"

"Of course you do, silly boy," the driver of the black car chipped in.

"Don't you call me *silly*!" I protested. "I didn't ask to be here. I can leave anytime I choose."

"Can you?"

I turned just in time to see my second companion from the car's back seat bearing down on me with a wooden cosh.

*

By the time I regained consciousness, darkness had fallen and one of my ankles was chained to a rail at the base of a metal-framed bed.

"Sorry about that."

I rolled my head to the right. Franky was sitting on a wooden chair beside the bed. He held out a glass of water with one hand

and a couple of pills in the palm of the other. I hesitated.

"They're only aspirins," he said. "I thought you might have a bit of a sore hcad."

I took him at his word and reached out to the glass and the tablets. My head *was* sore and I doubted aspirins would make much difference. It was worth a try though.

"I suggest you try and get some sleep," he suggested. "We've a long day ahead of us tomorrow."

"*We've* a long day? What fresh delights await me?"

"The less you know the better," Franky replied.

"*But I don't know anything!*" I protested.

Franky smiled and said, "Good."

*

I was shaken roughly.

"Sorry, young man, but we can't have you lying in bed all morning."

"I'm surprised I had any sleep at all. The

mattress has seen better days."

"Haven't we all!" Franky said. "Have some corn flakes with us."

"I might be allergic to wheat," I muttered unhelpfully.

"There might be some of yesterday's bread in the bin. Probably be a bit stale, though."

"I might have a wheat allergy."

Franky sighed.

"Well, you'd best hope we pass a

McDonalds," he said. "Order yourself carrot sticks and a side salad."

"Where are we going or, rather, where are you *taking* me?"

"You'll find out soon enough."

"I wish I knew what the hell is going on!" I exclaimed.

Franky sighed.

"Me, too," he said.

*

I was steered towards the big, black car.

My stomach was rumbling.

I was positioned between Frankie and another of the gang whose name I had yet to learn.

As the car moved away from the farmhouse and along the track that led to the road, Jimmy turned to the driver.

"You're sure you know the way?"

"I'm not worried about us getting there," the man replied. "It's the getting *away* that we need to worry about."

Several more minutes passed.

Jimmy twisted in his seat and half-turned towards the mysterious man to my left.

"It's time to touch base with Carlos."

"You want me to phone him while …er …" and he half-nodded in my direction.

Jimmy now twisted around to face me.

"You are going to be involved in a bit of harmless fun this evening."

My heart sank.

"How harmless?"

"You like art?"

"As in paintings?" I asked.

"As in paintings," Jimmy replied.

I fell silent for as long as I dared. The inside of my head was filling with bizarre thoughts. I knew this would be a stupid question but I asked it nonetheless.

"You want me to paint you a picture?"

"That's a stupid question." Jimmy said.

"I'd like you to look at some paintings, to study them with interest, and appear to be knowledgeable."

"And if I refuse?"

"Axel … convince our young friend that he doesn't want to refuse."

I had now discovered the man's name and after he had reached into the inside pocket of his jacket I discovered what it concealed.

If the sun had been shining that morning it would have reflected dazzling light off the shiny blade being waved in front of my eyes.

"Relax, Francis. Axel only strikes when he's angry … or occasionally if he's in a bad mood."

This had become a one-sided argument.

"Look, what do you want from me? I'm just a simple lad from a village close to Cambridge. I'm a peace-loving, reclusive person who would never intentionally causes offence or upset anyone."

Jimmy twisted his head still further towards me.

"All we are inviting you to do is visit an Art Gallery thirty minutes before it closes for the day."

"Inviting me?"

"RSVP. We'll even save you the trouble of doing that by replying on your behalf."

Axel stabbed the blade of his knife at an imaginary fly. "Got it! I never miss."

"Which art gallery?"

"That doesn't concern you," Jimmy said.

"Why thirty minutes?" I persisted.

"We'll explain that to you nearer the time."

I wasn't giving up just yet.

"Nearer the time on what day?" I asked.

Axel turned to face me and grinned.

"Today!"

At least one good thing happened to me that morning. Jimmy pulled off the road and drove into a service station. Half-hidden behind the petrol pumps was a *McDonalds* and, somewhat reluctantly, I tucked into a double portion of carrot sticks and a side salad. There were no gluten-free options at this outlet. It wasn't very filling but it was very cheap. Maybe I shouldn't have lied to them about a wheat intolerance!

We sat inside *McDonalds* as far from the windows as possible and Jimmy started to spell out a few things regarding the day ahead.

"We are going to drive to within four hundred metres of Duke of York Square in Chelsea arriving at around five o'clock. That is when your day begins."

My ears pricked up.

"Chelsea? Hey, can I call in at *Chelsea Music Publishing*?" I asked excitedly.

"You can do what you like afterwards," Jimmy replied.

"After what?" I asked hopefully.

"You'll find out soon enough," was his enigmatic reply.

*

We left *McDonalds* and the car continued steadily on its journey towards London.

I sensed my companions were growing tense and became aware that my heart was starting to beat faster. My smart watch could have confirmed this but I preferred not to know. The faster my pulse raced the more slow-moving the journey felt.

I watched houses, hotels and shops glide past but as I was not over-familiar with London, I had no idea where I was. If I'd spotted Buckingham Palace or Big Ben or London Bridge I would, at the very least, have had some idea.

I glanced at my watch. It was already approaching four o'clock and I really would have liked a nap. The thought passed immediately because Jimmy was talking to me again.

"Are you listening, Frances?"

I nodded.

"At five o'clock you will enter The *Saatchi Gallery* in Duke of York Square."

"I've no idea what *The Saatchi Gallery* is," I protested.

"We'll fill you in on the way," Jimmy said, "but first we need to stop off for you to get changed."

I heard muffled laughter from my front and rear seat companions.

My jaw had dropped, my mouth fell open and I began taking short, sharp breaths.

"Why do you think I took such an interest

in you on the train?" Jimmy said.

I wanted to say something witty in response. I didn't. I couldn't. I didn't feel jocular.

Fifteen minutes passed and then the car began to slow and finally pulled into a lay-by set back from the road.

Without turning his head, Jimmy called out to Axel.

"Would you get the stuff out of the boot, please?"

Oh, no! I felt my heart lurch.

40

Was this it? Was it here, in a lay-by beside a busy road that led to the heart of London, that I was to be murdered and my body thrown into a ditch? I looked to the far side of the layby and, sure enough, a ditch ran alongside it!

Axel opened his door and walked round to the back of the car. I heard the boot lid click and then some scrabbling around. Within a minute he was back. He sat down beside me. He now had a large duffle bag on his lap. He lifted it up.

"For you, Francis."

He thrust the duffle bag into my lap and I stared at it blankly.

"What's this?" I asked. It seemed an appropriate question.

Jimmy now took up the tale.

"Do you see the ditch at the back of the layby?"

This was it then. Curtains.

"Silly question. Of course you can see it. The bag on your lap contains a change of clothing - a *temporary* change of clothing. I want you to scramble down into the

42

ditch, change into the smart new clothes we've brought you, then neatly fold what you're now wearing, put it all in the bag and return to the car. Is that clear?"

I hadn't a clue what was going on but I nodded my head. It seemed the wisest thing to do in the circumstances.

I had nodded my head but remained rooted to my seat. I was too frightened to move. My brain said '*move*' but my legs said '*don't be an idiot, stay where you are!*'

"Carlos … would you encourage our young friend to get out of the car, please?"

'*Carlos*'. I now knew the name of my other back-seat companion.

Axel opened his door and got out of the car and Carlos '*encouraged*' me to do likewise by removing a small gun from the inside pocket of his jacket. A silly thought entered my head… so that's what the bulge was … it wasn't a packet of liquorice allsorts or cigars at all. It was a small gun … and it was pointed at my head!

Carlos smiled at me.

"This gun only holds one bullet but that's

all I need."

I got the message and scrambled out of the car, tugging the duffle bag behind me and then made my way over the grass verge to the ditch.

The men watched as Francis scrambled down into the ditch and out of sight.

"I hope he doesn't mess up," Axel commented.

"It's working fine … so far," Carlos added.

"Maybe when it's all over he'll write a

song about it," Jimmy remarked and the three men laughed quietly to each other.

After about five minutes and quite a struggle, I popped my head up over the ditch and shouted out ...

"What the heck is this?"

"Your emperor's new clothes," Jimmy said and as he did so I heard laughter.

I watched as he and his gang of cronies ambled towards me. They reached the ditch and stared down at me. I stared up at them.

"*Well?*" I asked.

"Well … it fits very nicely. You were an excellent choice."

"An excellent choice? An excellent choice for **what**?"

"An excellent choice for what we have in mind for you."

I dumped my own clothes into the duffle bag and handed it back to Axel who had an annoying smile playing across his face as he opened the car boot and tossed it inside.

"We'll stop along the way at a cafe close to our destination and you can take a good look at yourself," Jimmy told me.

"Doesn't he look dashing? "Axel smirked.

I remained grim-faced and silent.

"When are you going to tell me just what the hell is going on?" I said crossly.

"After you pass inspection," Jimmy smiled.

*

We continued the journey in silence. I could feel the tension rise and my heart was thumping ever-faster but there was nothing I could do about it. I glanced down at my newly-acquired black shoes, black socks and black trousers. The shoes were slightly too small and pinched my big toes. The trousers were black and tapered and fitted me perfectly. The white shirt felt a little stiff.

The outfit was completed with a cream-coloured jacket and green tie. The jacket had a badge on its breast pocket with a smaller replica on the tie. They both read *'The Saatchi Gallery'*.

*

The car continued slowly on its journey through London's congestion.

Finally, I found the nerve to ask, "How could you know these clothes would fit?"

I could see Jimmy's face in the rear view mirror. He was grinning.

"I spent quite a few days standing on Cambridge station watching who was getting on and off the London trains. I was looking for a suitable gent to fit the clothing that I had obtained from a helpful security guard at the *Gallery*."

"Helpful?" I asked.

50

"*Eventually*," Jimmy replied. "You seemed a perfect fit!"

"And the others?" I said pointing at my other companions.

"These unsavoury gentlemen?" and Jimmy swept his gaze across them. "They spent most of their time, *day after day*, in the station car park waiting for my phone call."

*

Within minutes, we turned into a side street and parked close to a sleazy cafe. Carlos got out of the car, put money in a parking meter, and then the rest of us stepped out onto the pavement.

I followed Axel as he walked towards *'Charlie's Tea Shop'* which looked about as inviting as a rainy day in Manchester. We entered the cafe and it made a rainy day in Manchester positively inviting.

Jimmy nudged me and pointed to a sign that read *'Toilets'*.

"Take a look at yourself if you can find a mirror that hasn't been smashed," he said. "Practise a welcoming smile and if anyone asks, say that you're filling in for Charles Wheeler who's not feeling well today."

"Charles Wheeler?"

"That's right …and I can assure you that he is *not* feeling well today."

"Why is that?"

"Don't ask!"

*

I stood in front of the mirror and stared at *Charles Wheeler*. He stared back at me. His face was drawn, his brow furrowed and there was a wild look in his eyes.

Then I realised that I was looking at my own reflection!

"Good afternoon. Are you enjoying your visit?" I asked myself. It certainly didn't look as though I was!

My new circle of friends had returned my phone but pointed out that they had downloaded copies of the photos they had used to blackmail me into my involuntary cooperation. I *Googled 'The Saatchi Gallery'* and learnt that it featured contemporary works of art. My interpretation of '*contemporary works of art*' might have been considered offensive to their artists. No doubt they might have thought the same of my songs.

Charles Wheeler was the gallery's principal guide, so the blurb told me, and I must admit his appearance was very similar to me both in height and in build. *I* didn't need spectacles but he obviously did … very distinctive blue-framed spectacles that matched his blue eyes. Was it mere coincidence or had James, or Jimmy, been drawn to my own blue eyes in his summation of a suitable stooge? Whatever, even if I was as blind as the proverbial bat, you wouldn't catch me wearing gaudy blue specs.

In all other respects, I had to admit that the clothes were a decent fit. The tapered trousers were the correct length, the white shirt's collar size was comfortable and was it a lucky guess on Jimmy's part that I took size ten shoes? I took a final glance at myself in the mirror, departed the toilets and returned to the alluring fragrance of sizzling fat and bacon. It would be good to eat but I didn't hold out much hope of appeasing my hunger. I doubted they catered for the vegetarian I had claimed to be!

*

"Ah, Francis, I'm glad to see you've returned, I thought you might have done a runner. Anyway, I forgot to hand you the finishing touch to your new persona."

Jimmy put a hand into the inside pocket of his jacket and brought out … *a pair of blue-framed spectacle*s. He must have seen my face drop.

"Don't worry. The lenses are plain glass."

Yeah, I thought. It's the *frames* that trouble me!

*

Well, I did get to eat. Charlie, after whom the cafe got its name, really did exist and he was as sympathetic towards my declared vegetarian needs as I could have wished. He conjured up cucumber sandwiches with a creamy cheese-yoghurt spread and I crunched away my hunger between slices of whole-wheat bread.

Jimmy kept glancing at his watch.

"Eat up!" he said. "We leave in five

minutes.

I didn't waste any of those five minutes arguing but simply got on with the job of satisfying my hunger.

"Thank you, Francis," he said as I pushed aside my plate and took a quick gulp of water from the jug that Charlie had thoughtfully placed on the table.

We all pushed aside our seats, stood up, and made our way back to the car. As we drew near, I heard Carlos curse.

"Flippin' parking ticket!" he exclaimed.

He looked at the ticket and then looked at their car.

"Front wheel on a double-yellow line?" he hollered.

We all took a look. By about three centimetres!

"Why don't they spend their time chasing real criminals?" he complained. *"Three centimetres*! Christ Almighty!"

"Just get going," Jimmy muttered, "we're wasting time. Get us to Duke of York Square in the next ten minutes even if it means breaking every speed limit and rule in the book."

*

Carlos did as he had been instructed and we were all thrown back into our seats as the car accelerated away.

"Ignore what I just said," Jimmy gasped. "Just get us all there in one piece."

According to my watch, the journey took seven minutes.

I am not at all familiar with London's streets but had known that the Royal

Borough of Kensington and Chelsea had been awarded its status by King Edward VII at the beginning of the twentieth century. Knowing this, however, did nothing to settle my nerves as Carlos wove his way through the late afternoon traffic.

*

My watch informed me that it was five minutes to five o'clock. My fast-beating heart told me to open one of the car's doors and leap out. Unfortunately, that wasn't going to happen because I was wedged in between two thugs.

I realised Jimmy was speaking to me after receiving a sharp dig in the ribs from Axel.

"The boss is talking to you," he grunted.

The boss was staring at me and drumming his fingers on his chest.

"As I was saying … remember, you are *Charles Wheeler*. You are wearing his uniform. The *real* Charles Wheeler is … *indisposed.* He was recently hired and due to start his first night's employment as a security guard at the gallery this evening but *we* have arranged for somebody equally knowledgeable and capable to take his place. *You*!" There was more …

"So … this is your first evening at the Gallery. The regular staffs are aware that a *'Charles Wheeler'* is joining the gallery as a night security guard but if they should catch a glimpse of you they will have had no advance knowledge of what you actually look like."

"So I won't need these horrible blue specs?"

"They took a security photo of him at his interview. He was wearing those horrible blue specs at the time so he … *you* … will continue to wear them *now*. Unless the gallery's director has a remarkable memory for detail he won't know you from Adam - or, in this case, the genuine Mister Wheeler."

"Okay," I mumbled. "Suppose I go in, raise no identity suspicions and smile nicely … what then? Surely the gallery will be closed?"

"That, my dear boy, is the purpose of you being there as its night security guard!"

*

I did as Jimmy asked. It meant I had no broken bones and could continue breathing.

I tried to remember all the instructions I had been given as I pushed through the revolving door.

I was confronted by a motley group of people who were lingering beyond the normal closing time. An American was speaking loudly to his female companion.

"It's a Van Gogh, you know," he drawled. "Isn't that right … *Charles*?" he said, glancing at my name badge.

"Er … oh, yes … definitely," I replied. I hadn't a clue. I wouldn't know a Van Gogh from a van driver.

"There, my little cookie, what did I tell you?"

The 'little cookie' smiled sweetly.

"You're so clever, honey."

At that moment, a voice called out my name.

"You must be Charles Wheeler. I've been keeping an eye out for you." A smartly-dressed, harassed-looking man strode towards me.

"We close in five minutes and then I will show you the lockup procedure. Sorry it's all a bit rushed but I expected you an hour sooner. Traffic, I suppose. Terrible at this time of day."

I nodded.

"After locking up, I … er …?"

"I will explain everything to you but, very briefly, once the premises are secure, you can settle yourself down on one of our comfortable settees and do a crossword, or whatever. I suggest that every half-hour you take a tour of the gallery to ensure nobody's come down a chimney and stolen one of our valuable paintings."

I was genuinely surprised.

"Will you point out the chimneys to me? Just in case somebody *should* try to gain entry and make away with stuff."

"I do not have *stuff* in my gallery, young man. I have *paintings ...valuable* paintings - which is why you have been employed as a guard responsible for overnight security. If there's anything else you want to know don't hesitate to ask Philip, our daytime security guard, who has kindly agreed to spend the first night with you and answer any questions you might have."

*

I was left standing in the middle of the room wondering what on earth I should do. Fortunately, *'Philip'* sidled up to me. He looked at my name badge.

"Hello … Charles. I'm Philip. I'll show you the ropes. Look, I know this is only your first night on the job but I have an awfully big favour to ask."

I was hoping he wanted me to go out and hunt down some more food. I was out of luck.

Or *was* I out of luck? Quite the opposite in fact!

"Did bossy boots tell you I'm off on a week's holiday starting tomorrow? I'm going on a seven-day cruise of Nordic waterways with my better half."

That sounded great so … what was the *'awfully big favour'* he was asking of me?

71

"You're off on a cruise?" I repeated.

"Too right I am. I aim to get a belly-full of culture that I can understand … unlike this lot," and he waved an arm around the gallery.

"Look at that, for example."

He pointed to one of the paintings.

"That's a famous *Van Gogh*, you know. On loan from Amsterdam."

"I know nothing about Dutch artists," I said, "but it looks pretty good to me."

"Pretty good? Pretty *expensive*! Worth a

fortune, that is!"

"What is it called?"

"'*The Potato Eaters*'. I wouldn't mind if somebody nicked it, you know. Save me looking at it every day."

"Bad as that, eh? Anyway, Philip, you said you'd like a favour off me?"

"Hmm … yes, if you would. I've not finished my bit of the packing and I always like to pack my own suitcase .The thing is, I said I'd pop round to my mum's tonight. Make sure she'll be all right while we're away."

"You want me to cover for you?"

"Would you? I can write down all the checks that need to be carried out."

I couldn't believe my luck!

I tried not to look gleeful as I said '*yes*'.

So it was that at around eight that evening I found myself alone in Duke of York Square, Chelsea, London, responsible for the protection of valuable works of art housed in *The Saatchi Gallery*.

*

The original plan had been for me to lock

the regular security guard, Philip, in the toilet block using Axel's single-bullet gun as persuasion. Having done so, I was to call them on my phone. The phone had been returned to me - but only after Jimmy had copied the explicit photos over to his own phone.

So what should I do now in the changed circumstances?

*

The first thing I did was call Jimmy to explain what had happened and receive fresh instructions.

75

"Well, that's a wonderful piece of good fortune, Francis. No guns, nobody hiding in the loos and a valuable painting awaiting our collection. Congratulations. You've done yourself proud!"

"I don't feel particularly proud," I said. "I feel like a criminal."

"But when this is all over you could be a very *rich* criminal! You'll get a cut of the proceeds."

"I'd prefer not to get *any* cuts, bruises or be *any* kind of a criminal. What happens now?"

"That's a good question," Jimmy replied. "A slight change of plan is required. Hang in there and I'll call you back in a few minutes."

*

A few minutes turned out to be almost forty minutes during which time I went through agonies of anxiety. I was glad of the gallery's toilet facility. It provided a comfortable setting in which to vomit and to clean myself up before the next chapter of this miserable saga.

While I waited for the phone call I spent

thirty minutes walking around the gallery and looking at some of the paintings being offered for sale. There was some really weird stuff hanging on the walls and the prices were unbelievable! I might know little to nothing about art but if I was about to part with a large sum of money I would surely want to know what I was looking at! I wondered what Jimmy and his boys intended to steal.

My phone played a merry little tune indicating that I had a call.

"Francis - is everything looking good?"

"Looking good? Nothing has looked good from the moment I sat down in the train at Cambridge station."

"Cheer up! Don't sound so pessimistic. Things are working out far better than I could ever have imagined."

"Whatever you intend to do, I hope it's over and done with pretty quick," I said.

"Have you spotted the priceless cultural artefact?"

"The *what*?"

"That's the description used by the

connoisseurs of great art."

"Perhaps you could modify the description to something I might understand."

"We're going to steal a Van Gogh!"

"A Van Gogh what?"

"A Van Gogh painting, you ignoramus. It's the centrepiece of the exhibition. Especially sent over from Amsterdam."

"Amsterdam?" I said. "You mean…like… from Holland?"

"How many *Amsterdams* are there, you ignoramus?

He'd used that word again. *Ignoramus*!

I fell silent.

"Francis … are you still there?"

"Yes, I'm still here. I think I might have seen it earlier. A group of people sitting around a table eating potatoes?"

"That's the one!" Jimmy said. "But not just *any* potatoes and not just *any* people. *Van Gogh* potatoes! *Van Gogh* people!"

"But it's not very colourful, is it? The people look so grim and the colours are so dark."

"My dear boy … I'm more interested in what someone is willing to pay me for the painting. I couldn't care less how they look or what they are eating."

I don't know why but I suddenly felt intrigued by the depressing scene on the wall.

"Hold on a mo…"

"Francis … can we just get on with this, please? A few extra minutes to you could result in many extra years in jail for us!"

I walked over to the exhibit.

"It says here that *The Potato Eaters* was Vincent Van Gogh's first masterpiece. He painted it way back in 1885."

"Great! So he's a very old man by now."

"He died in 1890."

"So he didn't have much time to spend his money."

"It seems he died penniless," I continued.

"Not something I intend to do! Now …"

"He cut off his ear in 1888 and then shot himself in the chest …"

"Never play with a loaded pistol. Now …"

"His last words were, 'the sadness will last forever'"

"And so will our prison sentence if we don't shift ourselves!"

That caught my attention. If Charles Wheeler, the gallery owner, discovered that he'd left his spare glasses in the gallery or Philip, the security guard, decided against going on his cruise because he felt seasick, we were in trouble. Particularly *me* because I was the only one here and I was impersonating a security guard dressed in strange clothing and wearing blue-framed spectacles! At any moment soon I would be helping to make off with a world-famous painting worth millions, no doubt.

*

I compared my complicated circumstances to the simple setting of Van Gogh's masterpiece. I wished I was sitting at a farmer's table with a family eating potatoes. My tummy was rumbling. I hadn't eaten since Charlie at the cafe had prepared my cucumber sandwiches.

"Are you still there?"

Jimmy's loud and angry voice awoke me from my thoughts.

"Yes. Sorry. What do you want me to do?"

"We're on our way. Check that all the alarms are switched off. Unlock the front door. The painting is not fixed to the wall. Lift it down … and be very careful! We don't want any accidents!

My heartbeat rose. I couldn't believe this was happening.

"You have five minutes to remove the

painting and carry it to the front entrance. We'll be waiting for you with the car."

"Okay. So where are we heading?"

The line fell silent.

"Are you still there?"

I heard a car's engine start up. Raised voices shouted to each other … and then the line went dead.

I felt sure my heartbeat surging towards what was probably a dangerous level.

*

87

The first thing I did was to unlock the door to the security room using the key that Philip had handed to me. I was trying hard to remember what he had told me. *'Press the button marked 'Gallery' and then the button marked 'Alarm'. Wait five seconds and then press the button marked 'Secure'.* I was starting to panic. Had I got the buttons in the correct order? I took a quick glance at my watch. A little over a minute had passed. It took another twenty seconds to reach the gallery that gave prominence to Van Gogh's *'The Potato Eaters'*.

I was too short to lift it from the wall.

I looked around the room and spotted a wooden chair positioned beside the wall furthest away from me.

I carried the chair across the room and placed it beneath the painting. The chair was slightly wobbly and I was frightened it might throw me off balance. I reached up and carefully gripped the sides of the painting's frame. So far so good. I tried raising it from the steel wire that stretched across its back and as I did so the chair rocked on its back feet. For a moment I thought it would tip and send me crashing to the floor.

The chair stabilised and I took a couple of deep breaths. This time I was able to remove it from the wall and lower it to the ground. I steadied myself and stepped down off the chair.

Roughly three and a half minutes had passed.

Carrying the painting towards the front entrance was difficult. Holding my arms wide, I gripped the sides of the frame and took small, cautious steps. I was almost there. I didn't know how much time had passed but guessed that it must be at least five minutes.

I was proven correct.

A large, black car drew up outside and I lowered the painting to the floor again and reached for the green button that operated the entrance door's movement. The frame of the painting caught me beneath my chin and dug into my throat. I gasped as my breath was taken from me.

Faces appeared at the glass window of the door and arms beckoned.

My next attempt was successful and when I pressed the green button the revolving door turned.

*

Axel and Carlos each took a step forward. Jimmy leant against the bonnet and Frankie walked round to the back of the car and raised the lid of the boot. He reached in and lowered one of the back seats no doubt making space for the painting. It occurred to me that there would be no room remaining for me! I had no intention of sitting on the roof so what was I supposed to do? Perhaps one of the gang was going to stay behind to see how things panned out.

Then a thought struck me. The rear seat had been lowered to create space for Van Gogh and his hungry potato caters. Carlos sat beside it with an arm draped across the top of the frame to hold it steady. Jimmy was in his usual place up front in the passenger seat giving instructions to Axel who was driving the car.

So, I asked myself … where was I to sit?

"There's no room for me," I pointed out.

"Well spotted, that man!" Jimmy

exclaimed. The other men smiled, opened the car's doors and quickly settled in.

Jimmy turned to face me.

"You understand we can't be seen hanging about here all night chatting."

I turned on him, my anger rising like a tidal wave.

"I'm involved in a criminal activity. I've impersonated a security guard. I've stolen a painting worth … millions. I've done all your dirty work … and you're just going to leave me here?"

Jimmy reached into a trouser pocket and pulled out a wad of notes held together by an elastic band. He tugged several free from their strapping and handed them to me.

"Call yourself a cab. Ask the driver to find you a room for the night, somewhere near Pancras Square. In the morning, you can visit your music publisher and sell him your songs."

"And then I suppose I simply return to Cambridge and carry on as if my world hasn't been turned upside down?"

Carlos called out.

"Boss, we need to get shifting."

Jimmy turned back to me and smiled. It was almost touching.

"I'll be in touch," he said and laid a hand on my shoulder. "You did well. You'll be rewarded."

With that, he settled into the passenger seat and the big black car pulled away.

*

I didn't expect to flag down a cab so late at night but I got lucky. I'd locked the front door to the *Saatchi Gallery* … after the horse had bolted …and I felt some sympathy towards whoever would be first to arrive that morning to open up.

The cab driver took me to an all-night boarding house tucked between a Chinese takeaway and a laundrette. I paid him using some of the notes that Jimmy had handed to me. I was able to get a room for the night and was led up a narrow staircase to a surprisingly clean and well-maintained en-suite bedroom. The only fault I encountered was attributed to the strong aroma of Chinese cooking from the kitchen next door.

*

I was exhausted. I was tired, frightened and unable to accept that I had been at the centre of an audacious theft. I crossed to the window and looked out onto the street below. There were a few old street lights dispensing a faint, eerie glow, a couple of inebriated youths and ... the wail of a siren from a police car as it sped past.

Jimmy had arranged to rendezvous with Duncan McDell outside *The Three*

Standing Figures in Regent's Park.

Carlos turned out of Turk's Row, onto the A3126 and headed towards The Lister Hospital. Duncan McDell was well-known on the dark web amongst a criminal fraternity that dealt in stolen goods and especially the works of art and cultural artefacts that carried high price tags.

"Duncan *does* know we're on our way?" Axel asked. "The sooner we get shot of this the sooner I'll breathe easy."

"You worry too much," Carlos said.

"We'll be there in ten minutes. He knows we're on the move."

"You think we can trust the lad?"

"No problem there. He's in way too deep."

Franky broke into a nervous giggle.

"Are we still splitting him in?"

Jimmy lowered his eyes.

"I'll take care of him. We can't afford to let him loose."

Nobody spoke for several seconds and then …

100

BOOM!

The car slew to one side.

*

Duncan McDell looked impatiently at his watch. The night-lights in Battersea Park had been upgraded and he had a good view of the entrance Jimmy would use to enter.

However, he'd now been waiting almost an hour beside *The Three Standing Figures* and during that time neither he nor they had moved.

BOOM!

The men in the big black car stared at each other wondering who had been shot. There was no blood, no cries of pain, no shattered windscreen.

"I think we've got a blown tyre," Carlos said as he opened his car door. The other members of the gang remained seated and appeared surprised that there was no blood, no bullets and nobody hurt.

Carlos returned to the car.

"Front tyre's blown," he said.

102

Jimmy rolled his eyes in frustration.

"That's all we need!" he complained. "We're already late. McDell was expecting us ten minutes ago."

"Not our fault," Carlos responded angrily.

"Well, fetch the jack. Let's get the spare on double-quick. We've a lot riding on this."

Carlos didn't move.

"For Christ's sake! Shift yourself!"

Carlos spoke quietly.

"We don't have a spare."

There was a stunned silence.

In a surprisingly soft and controlled voice, Jimmy asked,

"Why?"

"We needed the space for your pal's change of clothing. That, and his own baggage. Plus plenty of room for the painting and stuff to wrap it in."

Jimmy pulled out his phone and tapped in some numbers.

"Duncan. We have a problem."

*

Duncan listened to what Jimmy said and then put the phone back in his jacket pocket. He cursed, gritted his teeth and returned to his car. He shoved the car into gear and headed out of Battersea Park towards The Lister Hospital leaving *The Three Standing Figures* to speculate on his abrupt departure.

*

The sound of police sirens grew louder.

Francis began to panic. Had he inadvertently set off an alarm that had alerted police to a security breach at the gallery?

He returned to the toilets to retrieve his duffle bag but then remembered that it was in the boot of Jimmy's car.

He hurried back to the gallery and threw the security cap into a wastebasket. There was nothing he could do about the rest of his uniform. Running to the entrance door, he pushed the exit button. The door didn't open! He'd forgotten to override the security system. Running back to the control room he tripped on an upturned edge of carpet and was flung forward and onto his head. He rose to his feet, dazed and shaken, and stumbled his way into the security room. He deactivated the front-door switch and then retraced his steps taking care to avoid the raised carpet.

*

Francis felt free! *The Saatchi Gallery* was already fifty metres behind him and he slowed to a walk along the eerily quiet street. The silence was comforting. He set his mind to the day ahead of him but then realisation dealt him a hefty blow … he'd flushed Jimmy's notes down the toilet to distance himself from the crime … he had no money … his own clothes were in the big black car together with his recordings of two songs for the Camden publisher …

His thoughts were dealt a further blow as a police car pulled up alongside him.

"One moment, sir."

*

Carlos turned to Axel with a look of frustration on his face.

"We'll have to carry the painting. One side each."

"That's a bit bloody obvious, isn't it? You

don't think it looks a wee bit suspicious - two men lugging a Van Gogh along the pavement at three in the morning?"

"It's far too large to carry vertically," Axel said.

"We could call a cab," Franky suggested.

"The trouble with that," Jimmy explained, "is that we would need to silence the cabbie. Knowing our luck just now, a traffic warden would happen along and do him for parking illegally in front of the station."

*

Sirens sounded in the distance.

The men stood quite still and stared at each other.

The sirens had become louder.

"Well, I'm off!" Axel blurted out. "The cops'll have us in 'cuffs before we can carry this work of art ten yards."

"I'm with you," Franky said.

Jimmy half-turned.

"Carlos?"

The sirens were now quite close.

"They're right, boss. "We've failed."

'Failure' was not normally a word included in Jimmy's dictionary but he could see how hopeless their situation was.

"What are we going to do about the painting, then?" Carlos asked.

"Just dump it next to those railings," Jimmy replied, "and hope nobody steals it!" Jimmy waved his arms.

"Now scram. Separate directions. I'll be in touch."

"One moment, sir," the police officer said as he pulled up alongside Francis.

"It's a strange hour to be wandering along the King's Road, especially dressed as you are."

"I'm just on my way home," I stuttered.

"Could you confirm your name, please, sir?" his companion asked.

"Francis," I replied without thinking.

"Are you sure you don't mean Charles?"

112

Damn! I was still wearing the name badge from the gallery.

"I can explain …" I began to say.

"That would certainly be helpful, sir. Now, if you wouldn't mind taking a seat in the back of the car, please?"

*

Duncan McDell cruised past *The Lister Hospital.* It was two in the morning and still dark but the streetlights gave off an orange glow. Beneath one of the streetlights he could see a stationary car with one of its back tyres sitting flat to the ground. That would be the puncture Jimmy had phoned him about. He spotted a large, square-shaped object leaning against railings close by and pulled over for a closer look. Was he dreaming or was that *really* Van Gogh's '*The Potato Eaters*'? He threw open his car door and leapt out. Walking briskly to his estate car's boot he flicked open its lid. With a quick glance around the deserted street, he went over to the railings and dragged the painting by its frame along the pavement to his car. It fitted neatly onto the floor of the boot.

He tried closing the lid quietly but it needed greater force. He tried again and this time the lock snapped into place. He clambered back into his car and was about to drive off when another police car drew up alongside.

"You can't park there, sir. Double yellow lines."

Duncan's heart beat wildly but he managed to gather his wits and murmur a *'thank you'* before putting the car into gear and driving away.

He had driven no more than a hundred

metres when the same police car tucked in behind him and flashed its lights. Duncan slowed to a halt and his heart rate shot up again.

The driver got out and walked towards Duncan's car. He was speaking to someone on his mobile.

"Routine check, sir," he said. "We've had reports of a break-in at the *Saatchi Gallery*."

"Nothing to do with me!" Duncan exclaimed.

"As I said, sir, just a routine check. Would

you mind opening the boot of your car, please?"

Duncan broke into a sweat and thought about driving off but the policeman opened his door and beckoned with his torch.

"Do you need help getting out?" he asked.

Duncan stumbled from the car and walked to the rear of his car. He raised the boot lid.

"You're an art lover, sir?" the policeman asked. "Or are you the artist?"

"Good Lord, no! I can't paint."

"You're not the '*Vincent*' that signed this painting then?"

Duncan shook his head and replied in a quavering voice,

"No. That would be Vincent Van Gogh."

*

It was a busy night at Chelsea police station.

"Do you recognise this man, Mister McDell?"

118

Duncan raised his head and stared at Francis. He was still dressed in his security guard's clothing.

"I've never seen him before in my life."

It was a truthful answer.

"… but his name is Charles Wheeler."

"You just said …"

"Name badge." Duncan pointed at Francis' jacket.

"*That's not my real name!*" Francis retorted.

119

The officer on duty grinned.

"This is becoming more interesting by the minute," he said. "It's just like an Agatha Christie thriller."

"I can explain," Francis said.

"I do hope so … for both your sakes."

*

By the end of that morning, Francis had been released on bail. He was told that he might need to attend a court hearing if Jimmy and his pals were apprehended. Duncan was charged with aiding and abetting a crime but not with the theft itself.

'*The Potato Eaters*' had been recovered thirty-five minutes after it had been stolen although Jimmy and his partners-in-crime were never caught.

And Francis …?

His duffel bag was recovered from the gang's abandoned car. He was able to change back into his own clothing and the police provided him with a single ticket on an afternoon train from Kings Cross to Cambridge.

And his songs? Francis later posted a copy
of his taped songs to the music publisher
in Camden's Pancras Square but never
heard back from him.

REVOLVING DOORS

Cliff Morrison was 'one cool dude'. He
was idolised by Matt Reynolds and all-but
worshipped by Charlie McPherson. Both
modelled themselves on Cliff in every

possible way. They wore narrow, blue denim jeans, tee-shirts with '*I Love New York*' emblazoned across them and air-cushioned Nike trainers. Exactly as Cliff Morrison. He was *The Boss* and the words of *The Boss* kept them, most of the time, with a roof over their heads and food in their bellies.

This small gang of three spent many of their unemployed hours and days dreaming up all manner of weird and wonderful schemes to enrich their lives. Nevertheless, they failed to earn a steady living and relied heavily on benefits, food banks and charitable donations.

Despite their '*I Love New York*' tee-shirts suggesting otherwise, they shared a shabby, backstreet flat in Tower Hamlets, East London, financed with government and local council benefits.

*

Occasionally, they were each compelled to do paid work in order to meet government and local authority benefits rules and regulations and, when they **were** forced to work, their jobs never lasted longer than a few weeks. Between them, however, by one means or another, they scraped together the rent demanded by the landlord of their shabby flat.

*

The trio had been out together squandering some of their unearned income on alcohol. If nothing else, it made them talkative even though they had nothing new to discuss.

"I thought I might set myself up as a private sleuth," Matt mentioned casually.

"A *sleuth*?" Charlie laughed out loud.

"You wouldn't last two days as a *sloth*!"

"What's one of those then?"

Cliff took out his phone and thumbed through his apps.

"It says here … '*sloth - a slow-moving mammal that uses its long claws to hang upside down from tree branches.*'"

"That's you all right," Charlie laughed.

"Gee, thanks! I won't be buying you another drink tonight."

Cliff interrupted his two chums.

126

"We need to think up new ways of getting ourselves some more money without breaking too much sweat," he told them as they all sat around a table in the far corner of '*The Dog and Rabbit*'.

"That's more easily said than done," Charlie sighed.

"You mean … without having to work too hard for it?" Matt suggested.

"Preferably," Cliff replied. "In fact, pal, I'm already working on an idea that could have us sitting in the lap of luxury for a year or two."

Matt's ears pricked up.

"The lap of luxury? Well, I hope it comes with a cushion. My bum's getting sore just sitting here."

"What's your idea then, Cliff?" Charlie McPherson asked.

"Still early doors … but I'll tell you this … it could make us rich."

"Rich?" echoed Matt.

"For a while, at least," Cliff replied.

*

Cliff waited until it grew dark. What he had to do was best seen by as few people as possible, and *known* to none but himself.

He was alone in his flat.

Charlie was out spending some of his 'benefits' money at *The Red Dragon* public house and Matt had said he was going to argue about his credit rating down at the local bookies. It seems they had little faith in him settling his mounting debts anytime soon and wanted to have *'a quiet word in his lug-holes."*

Cliff tore a lined sheet of paper from the notebook he used to practise his arithmetic and picked up a pencil from the chest of drawers that he shared with Charlie. Matt had a cupboard all to himself in the small box room that also served as his bedroom.

Damn! Matt, as he did so often, had broken the pencil-lead trying to calculate the odds on *Fair Maiden* or *Mother's Pride* or some other in the *3.30* at some racecourse that was somewhere or other, but was doomed to finish last, fall at the first hurdle, throw off its jockey or simply sulk and refuse to start at all! His horses

might just as well have been *Red Rum* or
Arkle because whichever horses he placed
bets on was never likely to be placed.
Blaming it on the jockeys or the horses
was a poor excuse for throwing away
money!

*

Cliff used a kitchen knife to sharpen the
pencil, slipped into an old and worn black
leather jacket, and made his way on foot
towards the town centre. He had once
owned a *Harley-Davidson* motorbike and
the waterproof jacket had served him well.
It still did. He would still have had the

bike, too, if only he'd kept up with the monthly payments.

*

It was a cool evening but a dry one and Cliff covered the mile towards the town's shopping precinct in a little over fifteen minutes. He slowed his pace as he approached *Barclays Bank*. Most bank branches had closed, to be replaced by non-human machines that handled transactions but this one had escaped extermination. It was a pyrrhic victory for the residents of *Tower Hamlets* who had campaigned for months for it to remain open because the majority had no money to deposit and no money to withdraw.

Cliff was especially keen to note the entrance to the bank. It was something new to him. He hadn't come across revolving doors before - but then he hadn't gone looking for any! Tomorrow morning he would return and check them out. He would watch as customers entered or departed the revolving doors to the bank and observe just how they operated. There was no point in leaving things to chance and they were something new to him.

He'd never before encountered revolving doors.

*

"I've been looking for your pencil," Matt said without making mention of the lead he'd broken. "I've got a couple of certs at Sandown tomorrow and I wanted to write down their names before I forego them."

"When have your so-called certs ever won a race?" Charlie asked.

Matt looked a little shame-faced.

"Okay, I've been a bit unlucky lately but

134

conditions tomorrow should be perfect for my horses."

"I had to sharpen *my* pencil after *you* broke off the point!" Cliff snapped, interrupting his pals' conversation.

"Yeah, well … sorry, mate. I'll be more careful next time. Tell you what, though … I'll buy you a *box* of pencils from my winnings!"

*

'*City Vaults*' finished one from last in the 2.15 *Fitzdares Novice Handicap Chase* and at a little past 2.45 '*Glory and*

Honour' pulled up lame in the final fifty metres.

*

"What did I tell you?" Cliff asked scornfully early that evening.

"I'm short of cash and it was worth a try," Matt replied. "… and let me tell you, I was well on the money until *Glory and Honour* pulled up lame."

"Your brain pulled up lame a long time ago," Charlie added jokingly. Matt glowered at him.

Cliff couldn't help but smile at his foolish friends.

"Listen up now," he said briskly. "I have something important to discuss. With luck … not *your* luck …" and he smirked at Matt, "you'll be able to clear all your debts and even buy your own racehorse in a couple of days' time."

Matt and Charlie fell silent although Charlie still had a smirk on his face. Matt scowled at him.

"What d'you mean?" Charlie said.

"Wait until tomorrow and you'll find out. I

want you both to be here, in the flat, tomorrow afternoon at two. Is that clear?"

"There's racing at *Chepstow*," Matt protested.

"Not for you, there isn't," Cliff snapped.

"What do you have in mind?" asked Charlie.

Cliff smiled enigmatically.

"As I just said, you'll have to wait until tomorrow to find out."

*

138

"I have a plan to make us rich!" Cliff spoke quietly and he wondered whether his pals could hear the sound of his heart thumping.

All three were sitting around a small dining table in their living room.

"I've already tried that with the horses," Matt said. "It didn't work."

Charlie frowned at him.

"Quiet, mate. Listen to what *The Boss* has to say. Let's face it - he's the brainiest of us."

Cliff accepted the compliment with a nod of his head.

"I went out yesterday and again this morning to the bank in town. I wanted to check it out. I watched people going into the bank, attending to their business, and then coming back out."

"You watched people going in and out of the bank?" Matt asked. "Now why would you want to do that? Were you hoping they might toss you a coin or two?" Matt asked.

"Or offer to treat you to a cup of tea and a

bun?" Charlie chipped in.

"If you asked fewer questions you might get more answers," Cliff replied and then continued …

"One thing we must learn to do right is to negotiate revolving doors."

"*Revolving doors?*" Charlie said. "What the hell are *revolving doors*?"

"They're doors that revolve," Matt said and smirked at his flatmate.

"I know that!" Charlie retorted. I'm not thick, you know!"

"Whatever," Matt responded.

The room fell silent as they waited for Cliff to continue.

"Gentlemen," he said quietly, "we're going to rob a bank."

*

"It's too risky. We'd never get away with it," Matt gasped. "You *are* joking, aren't you? You're not thinking straight."

"We'd need guns for a bank job!" Charlie gulped. "Gotta have guns. I've seen enough films on the tele to know that!"

"No guns. Definitely no guns. Not *real ones*, anyway."

"Uh? Not **real** ones? What … are we talking about water pistols or something then? Bank robbers use guns with bullets. What other sorts are there??" Matt asked.

"*Kiddie's* guns. Plastic ones. Just to **scare** people a little."

Matt looked at his two flatmates and then back to Cliff.

"You're certainly scaring **me**," Matt said. "So what have you got in mind?" Charlie asked … and Cliff went into the details of his plan.

*

It was not a particularly busy afternoon at *Barclays*. So many people had now become accustomed to banking online that fewer members of staff were needed to handle the dwindling number of customers that still preferred to deal directly with a fellow human being.

The three would-be bank robbers pretended to be window-shopping but kept glancing surreptitiously over their

144

shoulders. They watched as a woman with two small children exited via the revolving doors and stepped out onto the pavement. The youngsters insisted on going back in … and out...and in…and out. They found the doors great fun!

There were no signs of fun on the faces of Cliff, Matt or Charlie.

*

The three men held kiddies' plastic water pistols in their left hands and both arms by their sides as they approached the revolving doors in a line. Cliff was slightly ahead of the trio with Matt and Charlie squeezed tightly together behind him.

Cliff reached out and pushed the bar that ran horizontally across the glass door. His two hopeful partners-in-crime blundered into the back of him.

"*What the heck, Cliff*?" Matt shouted out as he thumped his chin on the back of Cliff's head. "You might have knocked me stone cold!"

He raised an arm to rub his chin and in so doing his elbow struck Charlie's neck and flung him hard into Cliff's back.

146

The impact forced Cliff's head against the door and made him gasp as he smashed his nose against the glass.

"The door won't turn!" he muttered as he rubbed his nose. Blood dripped on to his hand and shoes.

"Just look at my trainers," he cried out. "I only stole them yesterday!"

"What did you say? C'mon, mate. We're drawing attention to ourselves."

"The door's stuck!" Cliff cried out.

Matt began to panic.

147

"Let's get out of here before someone calls the cops!"

Cliff was on the point of agreeing when he noticed a staff member approaching the door. She had a broad, welcoming smile on her face and grinned at them through the glass.

"People are always doing that the first time they visit us," she said. "You're pushing the door *in the wrong direction*."

It seemed not at all apparent to the woman that they were would-be bank robbers.

"Put the guns back in your pocket," Cliff hissed. "We've already drawn too much attention to ourselves."

The woman assumed that they had been attempting to leave the bank and pushed the revolving door in the *correct* direction to allow them out!

The gang of three were dumbfounded when they found themselves back out on the pavement once more.

Matt sighed with relief. He was thankful to have walked away from the bank unharmed, unarmed and free.

149

The three young men found a wooden bench to sit on in the shopping precinct that extended along the walkway opposite the bank.

"So … I guess we're not going back in. Change of plan, then? Back to the flat or down the pub for a drink?" Matt asked.

"We made complete idiots of ourselves," Cliff muttered crossly. "Well, I've got news for you - **and** them. We're going back in … and *this* time we're not going to look like a bunch of twits. *This* time we won't need any assistance from the staff!"

150

"I don't know …" Charlie muttered.

"*What was that?* Speak up!" Cliff snapped.

"Nothing," Charlie murmured.

"But before that we should dump our toy guns in a bin. If they saw us waving them around they'd think we were complete morons."

"Suppose we give them to some young kids," Charlie said. "Let them see that we're really good guys … whatever."

"*Idiot*!" Cliff muttered. "Look … over

there … and he pointed at a nearby litter bin. They took it in turn to dispose of their plastic toys.

*

"Look like you mean business," Cliff urged. "Here's what we do … we go in, line up next to each other along the counter, look tough … and then leave the talking to me."

"What are you going to say?" Matt asked excitedly.

"That's not something you need to concern yourself with," Cliff replied. "I'll do any talking that's needed." He stared fiercely at his companions but felt more scared than at any time in his life.

"*Okay*? This time we do *not* make idiots of ourselves when we go in! Crikey … it's *only a door*."

"A *revolving* door," Charlie reminded him.

"Yeah, well, we all know that *now*!" Matt grunted.

Cliff half-turned and beckoned them forward. Head down, he strode towards the bank's entrance at a brisk pace whilst his two companions struggled to keep pace with him.

Cliff paused for a just a moment, took a deep breath to help steady his nerves, and then pushed the revolving door in the *correct* direction. Charlie and Matt followed on his heels in single file. Once safely through the door, Cliff strode straight towards the nearest teller, a middle-aged woman with a bright smile lighting up her face and a well-practiced *'can I help you'* on her lips. Her smile grew broader when she realised who they were.

"Oh, it's *you* lot again!" she giggled. "I'm glad to see you managed to get through the door safely this time!"

Matt noticed that other staff members standing behind the counter were attempting to hide smiles behind their hands … and failing.

"*Hand over ten thousand pounds …*" Cliff ordered before adding, "*if you value your life!*"

The female teller laughed.

"That's very good," she chortled. "*Ten thousand pounds, you say?* That's an awfully large sum of money. Would you like it all in pennies?" She giggled then straightened her face before asking him,

"Are you sure that will be sufficient?"

"I don't think you are taking this seriously," Cliff said angrily. "This is **not** some practical joke! We're **not** playing this for laughs! You'd best take me seriously or you might get badly hurt."

"Ah, now, you're **really** frightening me," she giggled. "It sounds like you're **deadly** serious. Well, I'm **really** sorry to disappoint you but we've stopped giving

156

away money to people who don't ask for it politely."

Cliff stared at the woman in utter disbelief.

"You didn't say *please!*" she persisted.

"Did you not hear what I said?"

"Oh, I *heard* you all right. We *all* heard you, *right guys*?" and she turned her head towards her work colleagues who had, by, now, gathered around her and were openly laughing at him.

Cliff moved his lips to speak but it was

157

several moments before words emerged. He was feeling very, very foolish.

Finally, and for some quite inapprehensible reason he found himself drift into an American drawl to announce …

"I've got a revolver in my pocket, baby."

"Well, well! Let's hope it revolves more readily for you than our entrance door!" somebody shouted out.

This brought gales of laughter from a captive audience.

158

Cliff began sweating. This was *not* going to plan. He wasn't being taken seriously.

Perhaps he had demanded too much money.

"Okay! Forget ten thousand. Make it *five* thousand pounds and we'll leave and nobody gets hurt."

The would-be-bank-robbers had captured the attention of customers and staff alike. People were pointing and laughing at them.

"You think I'm not serious?" Cliff

159

yelled. *"Well, I'll show you how serious I am."*

Cliff ran towards a section of the long counter that had no glass barrier and leapt up onto it. He shrieked with pain as his ankle twisted beneath him and he landed heavily on one knee. He was sent sprawling on to the floor and at the feet of an amused audience.

Charlie and Matt watched the catastrophe unfolding in front of their eyes. Now in a complete fit of panic, they back-tracked to the revolving doors leaving Cliff writhing on the floor and attempting to reach up and grip the counter-top.

Matt leapt at the revolving door, arms outstretched, and Charlie cannoned straight into the back of him. *The door hadn't moved!* They were too panic-stricken to realise that, *once again*, they were pushing it *in the wrong direction!*

*

One good thing that arose from the chaos and ineptitude of the three men was that they no longer had to worry about the rent on their small, crowded flat. They were housed and fed in small cells … and all at *His Majesty's Pleasure*.

SEAN WHITE WAS NOT SO BRIGHT

Sean White made no secret of his vendetta against the police in Coventry.

For the best part of ten years he had escaped justice. Local shopkeepers knew very well that he was stealing from their stores. It was irritating for them, rather than costly when, barely into his teens, he would sneak into local stores and make off with a tube of *Smarties* or a *Mars Bar* or even a tube of toothpaste thinking he was escaping unseen. He was quite wrong in that assumption.

At first, he was more of a nuisance than making any real impact on a shop's takings. Occasionally, an owner would speak to the local bobby patrolling the shopping precincts but nothing ever came of it. The police was aware of Sean's activities but regarded him as more of a nuisance than a criminal. They had bigger fish to fry.

As Sean moved into his mid-teens he became more fashion-conscious and more audacious in his stealing and the police were forced to take a little more interest in tracking his movements.

As police foot-patrols began to wane, so CCTV began to come into its own as a means of *'keeping an eye on things'*.

Sean was becoming something of a celebrity on video footage and easily identified. He wore distinctive clothing, courtesy *of Marks and Spencer* and *Sports Direct* and usually wore a peaked cap that he thought made him more difficult to identify. He could not have been more wrong! He was easily recognisable.

At first, a policeman would call at his home and speak to his parents but they would simply shrug their shoulders and say they had no control over *'young Sean'*; that they shouldn't be held accountable for his *'pranks'* as they called his thieving.

Sean was not so young when he began

breaking and entering premises at night, though.

Houses and shops with poor security suffered. CCTV, when available, often *suggested* that Sean was responsible but there was nothing conclusive that could be pinned on him. The police had their suspicions, of course, and continued calling at his home to the point where his parents claimed they were being harassed.

Now in his early twenties, Sean felt the police were pursuing a vendetta against him and that the people responsible for that vendetta were based at a Coventry

police station not too far from where he
lived.

*

Sean stood in the dark shadow of a tree in
Roseberry Avenue, Bell Green. It wasn't
really necessary as it must have been close
to midnight and dark clouds were filled
with water vapour that clumped together
into raindrops and hid any remaining light
cast by a half-moon.

Opposite where he was standing was his
local police station …… and then the rain
began to fall which was a right pain

167

because he wasn't wearing anything to keep his clothing dry. If that wasn't bad enough he really *didn't* want to get his new *Adidas* trainers wet. He'd gone into *Sports Direct* only yesterday and tried them on. They fitted perfectly and would attract envious looks from his mates. He had asked if he could *give them a go* by walking up and down the shop in them. The sales assistant saw no reason why not.

That's what most potential customers did and Sean seemed a pleasant lad.

Well, Sean walked the length of the aisle and then turned around, began walking back more quickly, broke into a brisk run and straight out of the shop. He fled from the shopping arcade with the sales assistant still shouting at him from the doorway. That was yesterday morning. He now had tonight to deal with.

*

Sean had with him an iron crowbar that he'd nicked from his father's tool shed. His father wouldn't be missing it any time soon. He never did much work on the house. In fact, he didn't do much work *at all*! What was the point, he would say, when benefits paid more than he could ever expect to earn.

*

The police station was in darkness. The rain was beginning to fall more heavily in ever-increasing large droplets. He looked up and down the road to make sure that no one else was about, although how he thought he would spot them in the darkness was questionable, and then crossed the road. The police station was small and had limited daytime opening hours so he knew it would not be occupied. Those on duty would be stationed at their headquarters on the edge of town.

Sean was quite tall. In his newly-acquired *Adidas* trainers he stood five feet and ten inches. The fence he had to scale was six feet high. He stood back ten yards and took a run and a leap at it. His hands grasped the top of the fence and he managed to haul himself up and over before landing heavily onto soil saturated by rain. He would have to make time to clean them tomorrow. Sean now made his way to the rear of the building where he knew there was a window that he could scramble through. But first it had to be broken.

He swung the crowbar and smashed the glass. Surprisingly, nobody appeared to have heard the sound of the breaking glass or, if they did, thought it wiser to remain behind curtains or in their beds. A cat meowed and scuttled away into bushes.

Sean cursed as a shard of glass flew off and struck his cheek making it bleed. He punched a hole in the window sufficiently large for him to clamber through and then dropped to the floor. His wet shoes squelched on the floor but he was pleased that his feet remained dry. Good choice of shoes, he thought, especially as he hadn't had to pay for them!

He placed a hand into his jacket pocket and withdrew a mobile phone and began tapping out numbers.

"Hello, Callum, mate. It's Sean. I've broken into the cop station on Bell Green. Want to join me for a bit of fun? You'll have to get over a fence but I'll help pull you up."

Callum was never going to turn down such an invitation and within ten minutes the pair had opened plastic *Tesco* plastic bags and were stuffing warrant cards, radios and articles of clothing into them. To this they managed to add CS spray, batons, a whistle and a police utility belt.

After ten minutes, Callum decided he'd had enough and chickened out of whatever else Sean intended to do that night. He left the scene, pushed a police scooter to the fence, climbed onto the seat, and clambered back over the fence. He skedaddled, leaving Sean on his own and to his own devises.

*

Sean ferretted about for another five minutes before also deciding to leave while the going was good. He had sufficient sense not to push his luck further and scrambled back out of the window and into the back yard.

Once outside, he used the crowbar to smash the doors of two police cars, then walk over to the fence and trash the officer's scooter.

Content with his night's work, he once more took a running leap at the fence and scrambled up and over ... landing squarely in the bright headlights of a cruising night-patrol police-car. Blinded by the light, Sean swore to himself and covered his eyes. He knew the game was up. Nine minutes later he was at the central police station. The contents of his *Tesco* plastic bag lay spread across the counter and he was taken into custody.

*

Sean later claimed he could not remember breaking into Bell Green police station because he was under the influence of drink and drugs. However, police were able to play back CCTV footage which caught the 22-year-old clearly arriving at, and leaving, the scene. He was charged with breaking and entering, the theft of police property, damaging two cars and wrecking a scooter. He refused to name his accomplice and it looked as though Callum would not be called to account and face justice.

Sean still insisted his innocence even though, at 22, he had a criminal record stretching all the way back to when he was just 13. He claimed he had been under the influence of drugs and alcohol that night and not in control of his actions … but then some fresh evidence was introduced and events took a turn for the worse so far as Sean was concerned.

The scooter that had been wrecked was checked for fingerprints and the fingerprints clearly matched those of Sean… but unfortunately for Sean there was more …

It had been raining on the night he broke into Bell Green police station. He had scaled the high fence and landed heavily on rain-softened earth the other side, His newly-acquired *Adidas* trainers had left deep and clear footprints in the soil and they were a perfect match for the shoes he was wearing when the roaming police car had spotted him and driven him to the main police station.

… But unfortunately for Sean there was more incriminating evidence …

The police had found a dirty blood-stained handkerchief on the floor of Bell Green police station. In one corner, in bold red characters, were the letters 'S W'. Sean White felt a strong affection towards his grandmother and he prized the set of three initialled handkerchiefs she had given him the previous year as a birthday present. He had used one to wipe blood from his hand after a glass shard had made a deep cut in the palm of his hand. He later cursed his stupidity. The blood found on the handkerchief matched his blood group.

He should have worn gloves before breaking in through the window.

… But unfortunately for Sean there was yet *more* incriminating evidence …

His mobile phone had provided proof of a phone call to Callum at around the time that he had broken into Bell Street police station. The police traced Callum to his home address and he admitted to being involved in the theft of several items.

However …Callum refused to confirm that Sean was his accomplice. He was charged with theft and criminal damage.

Sean admitted nothing. Not that it made the slightest difference.

With so much proof of his guilt on offer, Sean's solicitor advised him to plead guilty to burglary and two counts of criminal damage.

The prosecutor, acting for the police,

outlined the case.

"Between midnight and 5am on January 15th, this offender and another forced entry into a police station. They scaled a 6ft fence and entered a compound before smashing a window to a temporary building and gaining entry."

"Once inside they conducted a messy search, opening 20 lockers and taking a number of police related items.

Outside, he targeted a personal motor scooter owned by Pc Dunne. He knocked it to the ground and smashed it with a

crowbar.”

The judge sentenced him to 20 months in jail.

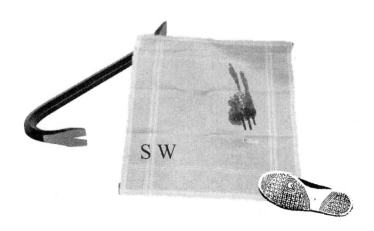

terry@terrybraverman.co.uk

amazon/books/terence braverman

updates: www.noteablemusic.co.uk

***

AVAILABLE BOOKS

(September 2023)

WHISKERS, WINGS and BUSHY TAILS book series (Stories from The Undermead Woods):

The Inner Mystic Circle

The Tick-Tock 'Tective Agency and the Case of The Missing Tiddles

The Mysterious Case of the Missing Scarecrow

Carrots

*****

Millie Manx (The Tale of a Tail)

Granddad Remembers (But is he telling the truth?)

Ninky and Nurdle (Stories from Noodle-Land)

The Playground of Dreams

What Can I Do When It's Raining Outside?

Buggy Babes

More…

CRIME

Time to Kill

Stage Fright

The Potato Eaters / Revolving Doors
(Fiction based on fact)

ROMANCE

The Man from Blue Anchor

A TWIST IN THE TALE

(Open Pandora's Box and what will you

find?) 25 stories with 'a twist in the tale':

A Night at the Castle

Baby Jane

The Christmas Fairy

Pressure

Baby

The Little Bedroom

Bulls Eye

A Problem at School

A Running Joke

The Cure

Old Rocker

189

190

The Doughnut Man

Mister Myson

☐

Printed in Great Britain
by Amazon